LOVE

Yearning Series, Volume 5

Ava Axton

Published by Ava Axton, 2023.

LOVE

First edition. May 19, 2023.

Copyright © 2023 Ava Axton.

ISBN: 979-8223614333

Written by Ava Axton.

Also by Ava Axton

Romance Wealth Series
SOJOURN TO THE UNKNOWN
PARAMOUR KING
MAVERICK CROWN
LONG LIVE THE QUEEN
COLOSSUS UNRAVELING
BUTTERFLY RISING

Yearning Series
ECHOES
BURIED
DARKNESS
BOUND
LOVE

Watch for more at https://www.amazon.com/author/avaaxton.

Table of Contents

LOVE

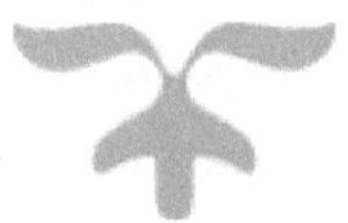

.. ⚜ ..

by

Ava Axton

Copyright

Introduction

Val thought she was the luckiest girl when she met Franko!

After years of hardship and torture, she finally manages to escape him and return to Cheshire.

Franko has just surfaced in town and is threatening her.

Val has no choice but to enlist the help of young and aloof detective James.

James has career plans and no interest in love.

Val comes to him for help. He tries to protect her and finds himself falling for her.

Her troublesome past is putting both of their lives in danger.

Can they trust each other?

Will Elijah and Sasha wed?

How much hurt and pain can the bonds of love fix?

Will love to prevail?

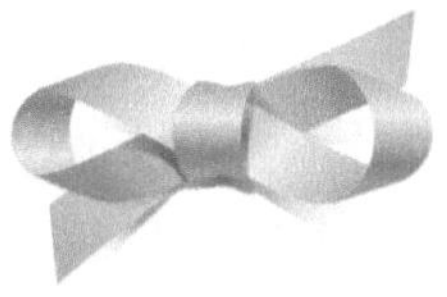

Chapter 1

Monsters of the past.

"This can't be happening," Sasha whispered, looking shocked. "Is anything we can do?"

"I can't believe he has the audacity to show his face after what he did," Kat said. "I am going to talk to Terry; I am sure he can pull strings."

"I don't understand," Josie said. "How did he even find you?"

"I don't know," Val whispered. "I do not know anything. I thought I had escaped him, but he found me-."

"This is the note he left outside your house?" Sasha asked.

"Next to the body of a dead cat," Val said.

She glanced down at the note that Sasha was holding, her stomach twisting and turning,

"I found you."

Just three words had been enough to shake the very core of Valarie's soul. One look and she exactly who it was from.

They sat in Sasha's bedroom, lounging on her bed. All the girls had hurried to Sasha's house at the moment Val had called.

"You don't have to worry about anything, Val," Sasha said. "You have us with you. All of us. We are not going to let anything happen to you, no matter what."

"Sasha is right," Kat said. "We are all here with you, every step of the way. I know Terry is going to do everything in his power to help. Believe me, Terry can help."

"I am sure Elijah and Jack will help too," Josie said. "I will also be there for you every step of the way. So will my baby, the way he kicks I am fairly sure there is a Karate champion in there."

The mood in the room lightened a bit, and Valarie laughed, feeling a sense of relief knowing she had all her friends with her. Plus, she had their men on her side. Each of her friend's boyfriends had promised to help her out in this situation. Val knew the monster they faced was not so easily defeated. She knew that despite all this help, there was little that could be done. She knew this monster could not be easily vanquished. He had wealth and power on his side.

"You know, I am also here to protect you," A familiar voice said from the doorway and Val whipped her head around. Hailey stood there with a tired smile on her face and a bright look in her eye.

"Hailey!" The girls shouted, running towards her, and enveloping her in a hug.

"I am alright, Girls," Hailey said. "I am so sorry I did not tell you girls about cancer. I just really needed to sort my own thoughts and feelings before I could talk to anyone about it."

"We understand," Sasha said, smiling brightly. "How is the treatment going? Come and sit down! Let us get you some tea and food-."

"I just received my first round of Chemo," Hailey said, sitting down. "It is a horrible experience; I do not recommend. Zero out of ten!"

"And what about you and Jim?" Kat asked. "You two doing it?"

Kat wiggled her eyebrow suggestively and Hailey rolled her eyes.

"Not yet," she said. "He has been receiving treatment to slow the progression of his disease and he has been taking physiotherapy to ensure his muscles remain in working order for as long as possible. They have been trying a new treatment on me. It has something to do with immunomodulation. I do not understand it well, but they said it has a much higher success rate than all the other treatments."

"Hailey, I am so happy!" Val said. "I know you and Jim are going to be okay. I just know it!"

"We all know it," Josie said with a soft smile.

"We aren't really here to talk about me and Jim, you know," Hailey said. "Val, I am sorry. I know you must be so scared right now."

"I was thinking," Sasha said. "You should sleep at my house for a while. We have a spare room. It is safer if you are with one of us, instead of being alone at your place."

"Thank you, Sasha," Valarie said. She felt very relieved that Sasha had offered. She had been dreading going back to her house. Ever since the incident happened, she had been filled with fear. Even the most innocent of things seemed suspicious. Every shadow made her jump, every noise had her scampering, while every movement had her trembling.

That man had tortured her for so many years. As much as she had buried it all in her past, she still remembered every single day she spent with him. She remembered the constant fear she had felt, and how horrible an experience it had been. Much as she tried to forget it, she could not. But she always had the assurance that she had escaped him. That she was finally safe and free to live her own life. She could not even imagine that he would find her and come seeking her again. She should have known he would never let her go.

"I think you should tell the police," Josie said.

"What will I say?" Val asked. "I have no proof. I have no evidence showing that he did all this. He was always careful not to leave any evidence that I could use. Even if I do manage to convince them to help, how long before he buys them off? He just might use his powers and influence to keep them from looking into the case. I have already been to the police about him once already. Even all those years ago, they had just sent me away. That I did not have any proof to base my accusations on. My bleeding head was not proof enough. No one at the station really wanted to go after him. He was too well-connected. Too-well known and powerful."

"I know you think the police can't help you," Hailey said. "But I agree with Josie. You should talk to them. The situation is different here. Please, at least try."

"Let me think about it," Val said.

She knew there was no hope. The monster of her past was invincible, and she might as well accept her fate.

Chapter 2

Shadows in the dark.

Val ran as fast as she could, her tired legs nearly buckling under her. She was going to be late, and he was going to kill her. The grocery bags bounced in her arms as she ran, trying to reach home before her time ran out.

"Be back before 9," he had said, and it was already 8.58.

She ran even faster, but her legs were starting to give away. And then, she tripped. The groceries seemed to fling themselves out of her hands, and tumbled onto the floor, spilling everywhere. He was going to kill her! That was all she could think of as she stumbled around, crawling on all fours, trying to get the groceries back in her bags. Her body trembled as she thought of him. Her fear of him haunted her thoroughly. She could barely think of anything else. It was all of which she could think. Him.

Her knees had been scraped and were bleeding, but she barely noticed. She glanced at her wristwatch, and it was already 9pm. She knew she was in trouble.

"Let me get that," A deep voice said, and she looked up to see the most bewitching pair of bright green eyes she had ever seen.

The handsome young man, dressed in an expensive-looking suit, kneeled, and picked up the scattered fruit.

"You are bleeding," he had said.

"Oh?" she gasped out, totally lost in his sudden appearance.

He reached out and placed a handkerchief around her knee, tying it around it.

"You might want to get that looked at, "he said, softly. "Get it cleaned and get some stitches. You might need a tetanus shot as well."

She was barely listening at this point. She snapped back into the reality that she was late. She was quickly scrambling to get on her feet and home.

"Let me take you to a hospital," he said, helping her stand up.

"No!" she replied. "I must get home. I am late! Thank you!"

With that, she ran back as fast as she could. Her only thought was what waited ahead for her!

Val woke up with a gasp, her body still shaking from the nightmare. The memory was so painfully acute. She trembled in memory of what had happened afterward. He did not like it when she was late. A reason wasn't enough to calm him down. He had taken it upon himself to teach her a lesson. She had never forgotten it.

She got up and walked towards the bathroom, splashing cold water on her face to soothe herself. She looked at her tired reflection in the mirror. Her brown mousey hair was messy and tied up in a scrunch on the top of her head. Her skin, complemented by a pair of hazel eyes, now had dark circles surrounding them. Val slipped off her shirt, and stood there, looking at herself in the mirror. Scars covered her body. Some appeared light and fading away, other more prominent and uglier. She remembered the torture and painful experience behind each scar. Her hand trailed down her stomach, where a huge, raised scar existed.

She remembered the hot iron he had pressed against her stomach while holding her down. The pain and agony shook her as she trembled at the thought. She could not let a monster like that take her back. She just could not go back to him, no matter what. Death was a better option than living with that monster.

Then, in the silence of the night, a scream rang out.

"Sasha?" Valerie shouted, slipping her shirt back and making her way down the stairs. "Sasha?"

"Hey, what's wrong?" she heard Elijah's voice as he followed her behind.

"I think I heard Sasha scream!" Valarie said.

They ran towards the kitchen, and as Elijah ran towards Sasha, Valarie froze. On the kitchen wall, written in what resembled red blood, was a message.

"Can't escape me this time!"

—

"Let me get this clear," the officer said. "You found this note on your front door, along with a dead cat. Do you think that the person following you is your abusive ex-boyfriend? Now, someone breaks into your house and leaves this message on your wall?"

"Yes," Val said. "That's what happened."

"Officer, what can we do about this?" Elijah asked. "How can we help Valarie? She is not safe right now!"

"Look, there isn't much I can do," he said. "I mean, I can look into the breaking and entering. I can try to track down the person who killed the cat and bring him in for questioning. But that is about all I can do at this point. You can apply for a restraining order-."

"Officer, this man is dangerous!" Elijah said. "Do you think something like a restraining order will stop him? We need to take some serious action! We have to find this man and arrest him! You need to put Valarie under protection-."

"Look, I really wish we could help," the officer said. "But as much as I want to help, I cannot. There is no proof, no evidence. We do not even know if it is the same man. Whoever this is, he knows what he is doing. I will investigate the break-in. Give me the information about this ex-boyfriend of yours, I can check his whereabouts. See what I can find. But that is the most I can do."

"Alright," Valarie said. "The man's name is Franko Ravasio."

"Excuse me?" the officer said, his jaw-dropping.

Valarie knew this reaction. That is how all the officers had responded when she went to file a case about him.

"I am sorry," the officer said. "There is no way I can track his whereabouts. Plus, this is a serious accusation to make against a man-."

"So what?" Elijah snapped. "So, because he is rich and powerful? You are telling me none of you have the balls to stand up and protect a woman from this monster?"

"It's okay, Elijah," Valarie said. "Just leave it."

"No, I won't," Elijah said. "This woman has had endured years of suffering and pain. That man beat her, abused her, tortured her physically and mentally. He tied her up and beat her senselessly! I am not going to sit here, while this man continues to torture her! He is dangerous, and he is going to hurt her! You know that! But you are all too afraid to do anything about it."

"I apologize, if that's the impression you have of us," a deep voice said. Valarie whipped around. In front of her stood a police officer, dressed in uniform. Valarie had to admit, he looked amazingly handsome. He was tall, well-built, with wide shoulders and thick arms which made his uniform fit well with his muscular physique. He had jet black hair, and his eyes were aqua, like that of the ocean.

He marched over; his eyes fixed on Valarie. Her heart started racing in her chest.

She caught a whiff of his musky smell and she swallowed hard.

He looked her square in the eye.

In that moment, Valarie knew she had finally met her match.

Chapter 3

The detective.

"Let me assure you; we will do our best to help in any way possible," he said. "My name is Captain James. I have been listening to your situation, and while I wish there were something I could do-."

"You can't?" Valarie whispered. "He will have you removed from the force if he has his way. You are all the same, all of you!"

"Ma'am-," James said.

"No, don't you Ma'am me," Valarie snapped, cutting him off. "Do not you dare Ma'am me! I have a name, Valarie. Do not forget it!"

"Valarie," James said. "Like I said-."

"You see this?" she whispered, pulling up the sleeve of her shirt and exposing her arm. "You see these scars? They are everywhere. I cannot even think of wearing a sleeveless shirt because of these! Do you see this one in the middle? He cut my arm with a heated knife. I was two minutes late coming home. Do you see this one? He stuck a pencil into my palm, just because he did not like the perfume I was wearing. Do you see these? They are all cigarette burns. Do you want to see the rest of them as well? Do you want to see the one on my stomach where he burned me with an iron? Or the one in the back where he whipped me senselessly because I did not make a good enough impression in front of his rich friends? I am not going to let that man take me again, Officer James. I am not going to let him even come close to me. If I must take matters into my own hands, I will. You, on the other hand, can continue to cower in the corner!"

She turned around and walked out of the precinct, Elijah following.

"Woah," he said. "That was intense. I cannot believe you told him off."

"I'm just so angry," she said. "I mean, I have been through this before. No one seems to want to help. Everyone is too scared to go after him, and I do not blame them. I mean, why risk your job and livelihood for a girl like me, huh?"

"You are wrong," he said. "It is their job to protect you. It is their job to keep you safe. Val, you are brave. When you showed me all those scars, I was blown at the pain you had endured. You are a fighter, you know that? Your more warrior than any of us. Do not worry, you are not alone. We are all by your side."

"Thanks, Elijah," Valarie said softly. "It's good to know I have friends like you."

—

"You bitch!" he roared, kicking her in the stomach again. "Do you realize how salty this dish is?"

He reached down and grabbed her by the hair, turning her face towards him. His disgusting face came into view, yellow teeth bared, a sneer on his face.

"You only have one thing to do," he said. "I give you money, clothes, jewelry, riches! Your job is looking after the food, the house and dressing appropriately when we are in company. That is all you

have to do, and you cannot even do that. You were at home all day, and this is what you made?"

He picked up the hot, steaming bowl of soup, put it against her lip, forcing her to drink it. She struggled, fighting his grip as she tried to get away, but he was too strong.

"You made this filth!" he roared. "You drink it!"

He threw the bowl away and slapped her face, shouting, "I am so nice to you, Val. I am so loving. I will bring you gifts and take you to all these nice places. Why don't you love me back, huh? Why do you act like this? Why do you do all this to me? I am not strict enough. Or you do not realize how good I am to you. I should give you to one of my friends for a few days. Let them have their way with you, maybe then you will see how wonderful I am!"

Valarie woke up with a gasp, a loud knock echoing through the house. She sat up, gasping and covered in sweat. The sun was shining through the window. She had slept through this morning. In fact, she had overslept without realizing it. She knew Sasha and Elijah would be at work, so she slipped on her robe and walked to the door, wondering who it could be.

She opened the door and saw officer James standing there, a warm smile on his face.

"What are you doing here?" she snapped.

"I am here to help you," he said. "I am taking your case, Valerie. I will do my best to protect you from this monster."

Chapter 4

Much needed help.

"**A**lright," James said. "So, he broke and entered this house and left the message. Of course, if it is him, then he hired someone to do it for him and I doubt finding that person will help much. The most important thing is keeping you safe. Going after Franko will not be easy. He has too many contacts and he can shut down the case within days. We will have to do this covertly."

"Alright, so what's that plan?" she asked.

"I am not sure yet," he said. "Putting Frank away on charges of abuse is not something easy to pull off. Frank has committed enough crime that if we can arrest him for this, we could put him away for life. I will figure out a plan, do not worry. Until then, let us keep you safe. I will appoint officers outside your house to keep an eye on you. Also, you are not to go anywhere alone. Do not answer the door if you do not know who is knocking. Do not trust anyone. Do not go to clubs and drink. Lock all your doors, get some security cameras installed."

"Can I ask you something?" Valerie said. "Why did you decide to help me?"

"Because of what you showed me," he said in a soft voice. "Because you have more scars than most police officers, and that's not fair."

He smiled at her, and she laughed at his bad attempt to joke. "It shows, the pain and suffering you have been through. Our justice system has failed you, and I apologize for that. I really do. You are very brave to have lived through that, and I salute you. If the man stalking is indeed Franko, your life may be in danger. It is my job to help you and keep you safe. If the man behind this manages to ruin me, so be it."

"Thank you for doing this," Valerie whispered.

"Can I ask you something?" he asked. "Franko?"

Valarie smiled sadly and said, "Yes, Franko. When I met him, he was handsome, young, charming, and rich. I had moved to Brooklyn to study, and that was where I met him. I did not know who he was or what he did. I just thought he was a businessman, and we dated for a year. To be honest, it was a wonderful year. He was charming, loving, and caring and showered me with gifts. Then, a year later, when I was completely head over heels, he asked me to move in. That is when things change. I found out what he did and could not believe it. Things got worse over time; He slowly became increasingly abusive. I thought I would never get away. Until that day when-."

She trailed off as the memories came back and she said, "I can't talk about this anymore."

"It's alright," James said. "I am going to back to the station and see what we can do. Do not worry, I have my officers keeping an eye on you. You are going to be just fine."

—

Valarie sat in her office, typing away in the dim light. She could not believe her boss had delegated so much work for her. She was sitting alone in the office, sorting through the accounts. Everyone else had left a long time ago. She knew James had asked her not to be alone at any time, but she had little choice. She had to finish this work today, otherwise, she would be in trouble. Plus, the building was secure and safe.

She quickly turned her attention back to work. Something did not make sense. With a sigh, she realized she would need one of the old files from the archives. She got off her chair and walked towards the archives. She walked through the box aisles containing dusty files. She slowly started to leaf through them. She had just found what she was looking for and turned around to leave, when a shadow caught her eye.

She heard the noise of footsteps outside and suppressed the urge to call out. It was just the janitor. She was not about to risk giving away her position. She backed silently into the dark corner, her heart racing in her chest. She reached down into her pocket, and she pressed the call button. After a few rings, a sleepy voice answered, "Hello?"

"James?" she whispered. "It is Val. Can you come to my office building? There is someone here?"

"What?" he asked. "What's going on?"

"I was at work, late and I had to go to the archives," she whispered, her heart racing. "I can hear his footsteps outside. He is making his way in here."

"Alright," he said. "I need you to hide somewhere, okay? I am coming for you. I will be there soon. Just keep a low profile. Do not make a sound!"

The footsteps started to get closer and closer. Val pressed the phone to her chest, trying not to make a noise. She really hoped whomever this was, would just turn around and walk away. She sat there, shivering and trembling, as the footsteps continued to echo. Shortly, they seemed to fade away and she finally let out a breath of relief. She slowly poked her head out to look around when a loud voice rang by her ears.

"Boo!" she lurched, half screaming. He had found her! He was staring at her, an ugly sneer on its face.

LOVE

Chapter 5

Nightmares.

She was running as fast as her tired legs could. She had to get out of here, otherwise, she would be dead. She briskly felt the rough grass beneath her bare feet, the cool breeze against her exposed skin. She pulled her tattered nightgown around her to warm herself. It was freezing cold out here. Her fingers were slowly starting to go numb.

She heard footsteps approaching. She instantly fell to her knees, crawling under the parked van. They were still looking for her. She could see their shoes as they passed by, looking for any sign of her.

"You see her?" a voice said. "The boss will flip if we don't find her."

"No, keep your eyes peeled. She has not gone far." the other man said.

She covered her mouth with her hand, worried that they would hear her breathing. They were too close. Any movement now and they would discover exactly where she was. She shivered as the cold wind picked up, getting stronger and stronger. She knew she could not survive outside in this trepid weather for much longer. She heard the search men walk away, and slowly bundled up, trying to conserve whatever warmth she could. If she got caught, she was going to have to fight for her life. They might kill her, she thought. Anything was better than being back with him, in that horrible place.

After a while, she started to calm down. The guards seemed to have moved away, searching for her elsewhere. She decided to wait for it out a bit more before finally crawling out of her hiding place.

She knew she had to make a run for it. She did not know how she would get through the main gate, but she had to try. The cold was making her brain groggy, and she could feel the will to live slowly slipping away from her. She huddled, shivering, and almost wishing for death to take her. It would be a better fate than what awaited her if she got caught.

She did not know when she had dozed off, but she was suddenly woken up by the sound of men around her. "She has to be around here! Check again!" An angry voice shouted. She cowered, waiting, and praying for them to walk away. They continued investigating and she prayed they did not find her. The men again walked away, and she felt relieved.

"Boo!" said a voice behind her loudly! She swiftly turned around to see a man's eyes peeking from under the van and looking straight at her. A terrified scream escaped from her lips, as she struggled back attempting to get out of reach. Two hands appeared and grabbed her ankles, pulling her from under the van. She dug her nails into the ground, shouting and screaming at the top of her lungs. She felt another pair of hands grab her waist and she was violently pulled out.

"See guys, I told you I could find her." a familiar voice said above her. Val raised her eyes and saw the familiar black eyes and that horrible smile. He sneered at her as she struggled and struggled against the men that held her. He laughed as he raised a gun and pointed it at her forehead.

———

The memory flash echoed through her mind, but this time; Valarie was determined not to lose. She slammed her head into the man's face, hearing the satisfying crunch of his nose breaking. As he groaned and grabbed his face, Valarie turned around and ran off, determined to get away. She reached the elevator door and pressed the call button.

"You bitch!" A voice shouted behind her. The man stood there, his nose bleeding and a livid look in his eyes. "You are going to pay for that!"

Valarie turned around, heading for the emergency stairs, and starting to climb down. The man was right behind her, following her as she ran.

"Come back here, bitch!" He shouted.

She ran as fast as she could, just hoping that James would make it here in time. If Franko's goon squad managed to get her, she was done! This time, he would make sure of it.

She reached the ground floor, threw the door open, running into the main lobby. She slowed down and froze. Blocking her exit were two large burly men who ran after her as soon as they spotted her. Valarie turned around again, making her way towards the back offices. She hoped she could hide there. She rattled the doors, but one by one, they were all locked. Desperation filled her and she took a beeline to the washroom. She hunkered down in the far cubicle and hid. Her heart was racing in her chest as fear coursed through her veins. She could hear them shouting and looking for her.

The bathroom window was too small for her to escape through. She huddled in the corner, hoping they would not come in. Tears streamed down her face. She could not let them take her back. She shivered at the thought of Franko and what he might do to her. He would destroy her, completely.

The footsteps got louder, as were their voices. Valerie realized there was no hope. There was no way she could escape these men, and there was no way she could escape Franko. This was for the better. No one else would get hurt this way.

Suddenly, the door of the cubicle flung open. Valarie almost screamed. In shock she acknowledged those green eyes, instantly lunging at the man.

"James!" she sobbed as she hugged him. "James!"

"Don't worry," he said softly. "I got you."

LOVE

Chapter 6

Peace for now.

"It was Franko," she said as he pulled her into his car. "He did it. He sent all these men-."

"Come on," James said. "We do not have time. We need to get you somewhere safe."

"Where are we going?" she asked, shivering.

"Somewhere that you can hide," he said, staring at the car. "The senior officials have refused to take any action against him. They ordered me to drop the case."

"What?" she gasped. "But then that-."

"That doesn't mean that I am leaving you alone," James said. "All those officers might be easily bought, but I am not. I took an oath to serve people and protect them from guys like Franko. I am not going to sit here, just because the commissioner has no sense of ethics."

Valarie looked at his handsome face, her heart swelling with emotion.

"I am going to keep you safe, Valarie," he said. "I promise."

"Why?" she whispered. "Why would you do so much for me?"

He became silent, looking ahead as he drove, and then he finally said, "Because I have seen marks like those before. I saw them with my mother. I was too little to protect her, and before

I grew up, she died. When I saw you in that station, begging for help, it reminded me of her. She died because no one was willing to save her from my abusive father. I was not going to let the same things happen to you."

Valarie looked at him, her heart trembling with emotion. There were tears in his eyes, Tears that he was trying hard to hide from her.

"Thank you," she whispered. "For everything."

—

"This is a safe house," James said, turning on the lights.

He had taken her to a small house, located in the valley outside the town. Valarie looked around the small, but cozy place. It even had a small fireplace, and the kitchen looked beautiful.

"You like this place, James?" A voice suddenly echoed, and her heartbeat accelerated. Could it be that James had betrayed her? Could it be that he had called someone on her?

"Levian," James said, flashing a smile to the man standing on the door.

"Valarie, this is Levian," James said. "He assists me in cases now and then. He is the one who arranged this safe house for you."

"Nice to meet you," she said, smiling at him.

"This is one of the most secure places I own. There is a voice-activated panic system set in place. No one would dare break into this place with my state-of-the-art home alarm system. There are laser sensors across the exterior. The moment anyone crosses them, it will send a silent alarm to Paul, head of security for this area. The cameras then instantly turn towards the intruder. There are no blind spots. The door has an automatic fastening system that ensures that no one can open it- either from the inside or the outside. If someone does manage to get in, there is a panic system set, which opens a secret staircase to the panic room. Besides, the guards will be here in a few minutes after triggering the alarm. My men will show you how to avoid the lasers-."

"What if someone else figures out how to avoid the lasers?" she said, cutting him off.

"If you had let me finish.... Even if someone does get that information, they need to go through a retina scan to get inside the house. Now, shall we all go in?"

Valarie walked inside, with James slowly following close behind her. The next few minutes were spent walking her through the required security information. Finally, Levian left, leaving her alone with James.

"Your friend is quite a character," she said, smiling at him.

"Yes, I know. I am starting to wonder what is it about me that tends to attract weirdos? I mean first Levian and now you-." he said, a grin on his face.

She punched him lightly, laughing at how at ease she suddenly felt around him.

"Thank you, James, thank you for helping me. I would be dead right now if you had not come for me. You went out of your way, and I cannot thank you enough." she said, feeling her eyes water. She did not know why but standing there in that small cottage, her heart suddenly felt heavy. She had never thought that she would ever be able to sleep peacefully again. Tonight, she could finally close her eyes and feel some degree of safety. The man in front of her was the reason for it.

"Alright, no need to get all emotional-." James said. Without thinking, overcome with emotion, Valerie leaned over and kissed him.

The moment her lips pressed against his firm ones; a shiver ran down her spine. She took in those blissful seconds. The way his lips melded against hers, like a puzzle piece, perfectly. Oh! The tenderness of his arms wrapped around her and the passionate euphoria that exploded through her body! How exciting his chest felt as she traced her fingers over his muscles. The fire that ignited deep in her soul now ignited, would not go out.

She never wanted the kiss to stop. A minute later, he pulled himself away.

"I should go." he said softly.

Her heart had a painful pang, but she smiled and backed off.

"Okay," she said, softly.

"It's just, I have an early day at work tomorrow and I really need to get some rest." he said.

"Alright," she whispered. "Thank you for all the help."

"I will check up on you as soon as I get free." he said, quickly. "You will be safe here. Levian agreed to give up one of his men to keep an eye on the place. If anything happens, I will be here immediately."

She gave him a small smile and nod, her heart feeling heavy and tired.

"I guess I will see you tomorrow?"

"I guess."

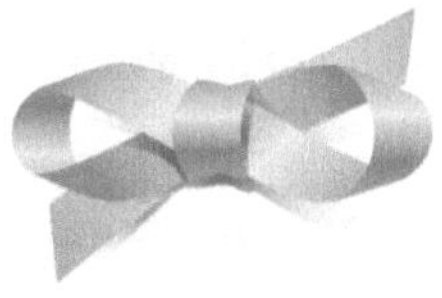

Chapter 7

Matters of the heart.

James was bleeding and limping as he ran through the secluded area. While leaving work a bunch of men had suddenly attacked him. He had little doubt that the men belonged to Franko. He did not know how, but he managed to fight off the assault and make it to his car. The rush of adrenaline played a hug role in it. He drove non-stop to the hideout, worried that the person who sent those men after him had also managed to track down Valarie. He stumbled over the grass, trying to avoid the laser sensors as best he could. A quick eye scan finally opened the door; he barged in and was instantly greeted by a blood curdling scream.

"What the hell are you doing?" Val shouted, breathing hard. "You scared me!"

"Sorry," he said sarcastically, collapsing on the sofa. "I didn't mean to scare you." I just needed to make sure you where ok, after what I just went through. I just have a few minor scratches, but I had to make sure you were OK."

"What? You are bleeding." she said, rushing over to inspect James.

"I am sorry," James said, rolling his eyes. She smacked his arm in response and slowly started to examine the bruises and the gaping wound in his shoulder.

"What happened?" she said, running off to find a first aid kit.

"I thought there was someone tailing my car on my way back from the station. I managed to shake them off; or so I thought. When I reached back to my apartment, two men were waiting for me. I still do not know how I managed to fight them off. I barely managed to get in the car and drive away."

"God, those bruises look bad. I do not even know what to do about that wound. I think we should ask Levian to send a doctor." Valerie said.

"No. He has helped enough by providing this house and the guards. He did all this because he owes me a favor. I do not want to bother him with asking him for anymore of his people." he said, grimacing in pain.

"This is going to need stitches. The wound is deep, and I do not know if can fix it. I cannot barely get the bleeding in control."

"Don't worry about it," he mumbled, his vision slowly starting to dim.

"James?" Val said, lightly slapping his cheeks. "James? Stay with me. James?"

"Very sleepy," he whispered, his eyes half-closed.

"James? I need you to stay awake." he could hear her voice echoing, as if in the distance.

"Sorry-," he mumbled before his vision went blurry and he blacked out.

—

"James?" Valarie shouted. "James?"

She watched as his eyes fluttered open, and he finally regained consciousness.

"I am fine, Val. Thank you." he whispered, sitting up.

"I did the best I could with the wound. Are you sure we cannot get Levian to send a doctor?" Valarie said, softly. Her hand was resting on his, and strangely, it comforted him.

He shook his head as he laid back down.

"I am alright, Val," he said, giving her a reassuring smile.

"I am going to get you some food. I made some soup with roasted chicken."

"Sounds fancy."

"Levian had one of his men drop some groceries off today," Val said, before getting up and heading to the kitchen.

"I made a quick evaluation of your injuries. Thankfully, none of your ribs feel fractured. There is some severe bruising, some minor internal bleeding, but I cannot be sure. The most pressing issue was the wound on your shoulder, which I managed to somehow bandage up." she said.

Valarie pensively said softly, "This happened to you because of me, didn't it? He sent those men after you because somehow, he found out that you helped me. I am sorry to involve you in all this." said Val.

"Val do not think like that. You were in danger, and you did what you thought best. I am glad that you came to me and that I was able to do something." James said.

Her shoulder started to shake as tears started to fall down her eyes.

"Val? What is wrong?" he asked, walking over, and standing behind her. She turned around and looked at him, tears streaming down her cheeks.

"I am the reason this happened to you. Now he is after you as well, and he will not stop coming after you. I ruined your life because I was too selfish. I only thought about myself and did not even consider how it would affect you."

"That is not true. You came to me for help. You asked me and I made the decision to do it. This was my choice, not yours. Do not blame yourself for any of this. I would rather go through this than find out that something happened to you because I did not help."

He raised his thumb and slowly wiped the tears off her smooth cheek. She looked into his eyes, and for a second, she found it hard to breathe. There was something so mesmerizing, so fascinating about his eyes, that she could not look away. The raw emotion that shone through his eyes shook her. She took a step closer, acutely aware of his presence. Her entire skin was tingling, and she kept feeling a strong, gravitating pull towards him.

Standing here in front of each other, bearing all emotions and their hearts, made her feel strangely connected to him. She leaned forward and softly pressed her lips against his. She did not have to wait long for his response, a second later he kissed her back. Valarie felt his firm and tender lips pressed against hers, igniting in her body emotions she had never felt before. She trembled as he took charge, pressing her body to the wall and kissing her passionately and hungrily.

The shrill ringing of his phone interrupted them, and they broke away, gazing into each other's eyes.

"I have to take this," he said. He picked up the phone and walked away, and Valarie called Sasha to let her know that she was safe. As she ended the call, she turned around and found James standing there, with a huge smile on his face.

"That was the FBI," he said with a grin. "They have agreed to help us catch Franko. The chase is now on."

35

Chapter 8

Truth.

"You know," she whispered. "If I had any idea when I met him, that this was the kind of man he was, I would have run away screaming."

"Well, dating the leader of the Russian mafia is definitely not an ideal situation," he said with a smirk.

"I had no idea," she said. "I thought he was just a charming gentleman. I dated him, and he was so loving and caring. Then one day, I overheard him talking to one of his men. Until then, I had no idea what it was he did. I just thought he was a businessman. But when I heard him talking about trafficking humans and sex slaves. I was shocked. I did not know what to do or say. By the time it hit me that I should run away, one of his men caught me eavesdropping at the door. He dragged me into his office. I still remember how livid he looked. He told me that this was the end for me. That I would never be able to escape him now. Now that I knew the truth about him and would have to stay with him forever."

"Then he took you to his estate?" James guessed.

"Yes," she said. "There guards always watched me. Not allowed to go far or do anything. That was also when he started to show his true colors. He became abusive, beating me, burning me, whipping me. He tortured me mentally and physically, mainly because it was fun for him. It was the most horrible time of my life. I do not know how I survived. I thought I was going to die in there. Then, one day, I saw an opportunity to escape. I convinced one of his servant girls to help me. She brought me the key to the door when she brought me my meal. I managed to get out, and remember running through his estate, cold and trembling. I hid under one of the cars, but they found me. They were going to take me back to him, but something urgent happened. Someone had tipped the police off about the sex trafficking, and there was a raid. In a panic, they dropped me, and I ran away, as fast as I could. Eventually, I collapsed too exhausted to continue, passed out on the streets. A kind old couple found and nursed me back to health. I then quickly returned to this town. I thought my past was finally all behind me but-."

"But he found you," James said. "Franko is not the kind to let things like this go easily. The fact that you escaped makes you lose. That hurt his ego. Which explains why he wants you back."

"After the escape," Valarie whispered. "I went to the police, and I told them what had happened, but they all refused to take affirmative action. Ever since the raid, Franko had pulled some 'deep strings' to keep the police out of his business. He paid off some higher-ups, and in return, they promised not to take any action against him. When you decided to help, I just could not believe it-."

"How could I not help you?" he said, grinning. "When I met you, I must admit, I was instantly taken in by you. I thought you were sassy, and beautiful, and confident. But then when I saw your scars, I realized I could not abandon you. Even if it meant going against my own seniors."

"But now we are going to stop him, right?" she asked. "Now it's all going to end, right?"

"Yes," he said. "The FBI has agreed to build an operation against him. But you are not going to like it much."

"What?" she asked. "Why?"

"The FBI wants to use you as bait," James said. "They want me to pretend to betray you and give you up to him. You will be wired of course. Once you are in his clutches; they will use the chance to send their squad in for an arrest. It is the only way we can pull this off. But it is risky, Val. You do not have to do this. It will not be easy, and this could go seriously wrong."

"I know," Valarie said. "If it means he goes away to prison for good, I will do it. I have spent a long time living in fear of him. If we do not do this now, I will continue living in fear of him. Besides, when I ran away from that place, I felt guilty. I was guilty because of all the girls I was leaving behind. He has girls there he has kidnapped from families that have no clue their whereabouts. I cannot let this injustice happen any longer. I will do it."

James looked at her, his eyes brimming with emotion.

"You are a brave woman, Valarie," he whispered. "I am proud to have met you."

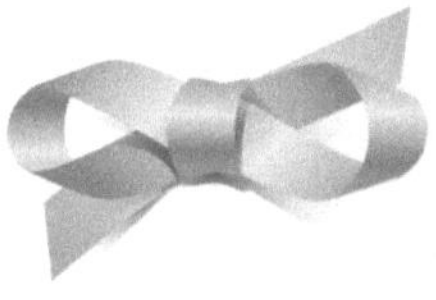

Chapter 9

The chase.

"Alright," James whispered. "Is everyone in place?"

A voice erupted from the walkie-talkie, "All teams are GO. Move on with the plan."

"Val are you sure you want to do this?" he whispered. "If anything goes wrong, you will be in his clutches again. This time, he may not let you go again."

"I know," she whispered. "I am so scared, James. But if I do not do this now, who knows how many more girls will suffer. I must do this."

"Alright," he said. "We are going in."

He started the car and drove down to the estate that Valarie remembered - one that terrified her. She had so many memories of this place, and every single one of them horrified her.

He drove through the main gate, which automatically swung open and then on to the main house.

She could see Franko standing there, a smirk on his face as he watched her appear. He had not changed even a bit. He was still just as handsome features that had caught her eye those years ago. But only now she could see the sharp and ugly glint in his eyes.

"You thought you could get away from me, didn't you?" he said as James dragged her out of the car. "Truly, you underestimated Franko, Valarie."

James threw her on the floor, and said, "I got her as I promised. I want my money now."

"Take her," Franko said to one of his guards. "Take her to my room and keep her there. I will deal with her myself."

"Come on!" one of the guards said, grabbing her and dragging her inside. She turned around and her eyes met James, who was looking at her with concern. Seeing him standing there, so strong, and brave, reassured her and comforted her. As they dragged her inside, his face was the last thing she saw before the doors shut in her face.

The guard dragged her inside, all the way to Franko's room. The moment she was inside his room, she knew what to do. She swiftly pulled out the taser that James had hidden under her clothes and tasered the guard until he collapsed unconscious. The next part was risky, and if she got caught, it would mean the end of her and the entire operation.

She got out of the room, sneaking around the guards, sticking to the shadows. She knew she just had to get to the kitchen, into the pantry, and her job was done. She made her way past the guards, staying hidden and just praying that they did not spot her. If she got caught, there would be no way out. She knew that. She knew that if Franko got his hands on her, he would never let her go. The entire FBI operation would fail.

The FBI had tried to get Franko before. Somehow, he had found out, and cleared out and trace of his criminal enterprise. This time, the FBI was working on a smaller version of their old operation, with a more trusted team. For this to work, they needed someone inside Franko's home. That is where Valerie came in to play.

She snuck into the kitchen, her heart pounding in her chest. There were people around and she was almost certain she would get caught. Her heart shook at the thought of being found out, but she plodded on.

She had escaped him all those years ago and had lived with the guilt that she had deserted all the girls he had kidnapped and kept here. She wished that she could have taken them all with her that day. That had really bothered her. Her friends had convinced her that she just had to get out of that town and disappear. But the guilt remained. Now, she had a chance to make things right, she was not going to back out.

"Excuse me?" one of the maids said. "What are you doing here?"

"Uhm-," Valarie stammered. "I am Franko's new mistress, and I want to see the pantry. I want to see how you run things around here. I must make sure everything is run properly."

"But I haven't seen you before," the maid said, frowning.

"If you are going to defy me like this," Valatie said. "Then I am going to have a personal word with Franko about your employment here. What is your name, girl?"

"I-," the maid stammered.

"I want you to take me to the pantry. Or else!" Valarie ordered. As the maid turned around and started to guide her, Valarie felt relieved. She walked into the small room and said, "Get out!"

"But-," the maid stammered.

"Do you want to keep working here?" Valarie said. "Get out!"

The maid finally retreated but Valarie knew that she was suspicious. The maid was running off to tell one of the guards right now. A distant shout echoed. Val knew that the guard she had tasered had been found. The guards would be here within seconds. She quickly set up the C4 and explosive charges that the FBI had taped on her body, under her clothes. She pulled them off her, setting them the way she had been taught. The pantry was connected to an underground tunnel, which the FBI was going to use to sneak in. They were already waiting on the other side.

"Hey, you!" The guards shouted. "Get here!"

Valarie felt panic coursing through her. She had to set off the charges, otherwise, this all was for naught.

"We know you are with the police," the guard said. "We got that boyfriend of yours as well! We know you were in on the plan with him!"

As the guard grabbed her, her thumb rested on the remote trigger switch.

The FBI had warned her to make sure that she was out of range before exploding the ordinance, but she was out of time. If they had James, then his life would be in danger. They would kill him! He might already be dead.

Valarie closed her eyes and thought of the handsome man who had put so much on the line for her. He had put his own life in danger to help her, and she knew she could not desert him.

She took a deep breath and pressed the trigger.

LOVE

45

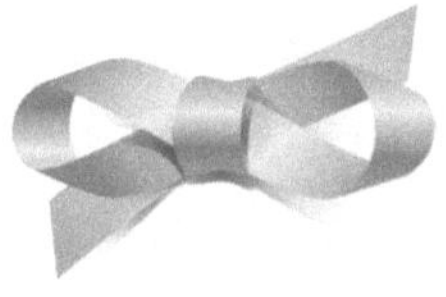

Chapter 10

The wedding.

"Oh God," Valarie said, tears in her eyes. "I do not believe this. This cannot be happening."

Sasha looked back into her eyes, trying hard to keep her tears at bay.

"What do you think?" Sasha whispered.

"Absolutely ethereal," Valarie whispered.

Sasha stood in front of her, dressed in her wedding gown, her long veil cascading down her back.

"Oh, don't make me cry," Sasha whispered. "I have got my makeup on!"

"I can't believe you are getting married today!" Valarie said.

"Oh, girls!" Hillary said, tears in her eyes. "I can't believe this is happening!"

"We can have an emotional moment afterwards," Kat said. "We are late. The bridal entrance was supposed to be two minutes ago-."

The door burst open, and Josie ran in, fixing up her hair. "I am so sorry I am late. The baby threw up last minute and-."

She trailed off as she looked at Sasha standing there.

"Oh, wow," Josie whispered. "You look so lovely. I cannot believe this is happening."

"I can't believe it either!" Sasha said. "What about Elijah? Did you see him? Is he standing out there?"

"Yes, he is," Valarie said. "And I must say he looks rather handsome."

"Are you sure I am not making a mistake?' Sasha whispered.

"You love Elijah," Valarie whispered. "And he loves you. Do you realize how rare that is? I am so glad that you found love in your life, Sasha. I am so glad that you are happy."

"Alright, time to go," Sasha said, and Valarie offered her friend her arm. Not having her father walk Sasha down the aisle, Valarie had offered to do it. The two friends walked out of the room and onto the wedding hall, where Elijah stood waiting. He looked handsome and proud as he gazed down at the woman that was to be his wife. The guests all smiled down, and Valarie spotted James standing in the back row. He winked at her, and Valarie smiled back.

The wedding march began to play, and Valarie slowly led her friend down the aisle. She smiled as she saw Elijah tear up, and her heart swelled with happiness. Elijah pulled out his handkerchief to wipe his eyes and Valarie wondered how it felt. To love so much. To love so intently.

"I love you," Valarie said to Sasha, kissing her cheek before walking away. Sasha stood across from Elijah, while the preacher began the ceremony.

"Have you prepared your vows?" he asked.

Elijah cleared his throat looking at Sasha and said, "You are the light of my life, Sasha. Before you walked in my life, I was breathing. I was moving through life mechanically. Not really enjoying it. Not there. Then, I met you and everything changed. I started to live! I started to want to live! You filled me up with a soul and spirit that made me feel alive. I never thought I could feel so much love for one person. I never thought I was deserving enough to be loved. But you Sasha, you changed everything. You gave me love I never thought I would feel. I am the luckiest man to have you in my life. I vow to spend the rest of my life showing you exactly how much I love you, every single day."

Sasha sniffed, tears falling down her cheeks.

"Elijah," she whispered. "I had such a long speech prepared, but I really do not think I can say it. There is no way I could say anything more beautiful than what you said. You not only talked of your own heart but my heart. So, I will just say this, I love you, Elijah. You are a gem of a person. Even if I had spent the rest of my life looking for anyone remotely as good as you, I would fail. You are like heaven on Earth. I wish I could say you are everything I dreamed of, but I cannot. You are a lot more. I could not even have imagined a man as good and as perfect as you in my life. You are more than what I wanted. You were who I needed. I love you, Elijah. I always have. I always will."

Valarie barely heard the rest of the ceremony; she was so overcome with emotion. The preacher pronounced them husband and wife, and the happy couple kissed. Valarie clapped and cheered as her sister beamed down at everyone.

"Care to dance?" James said appearing behind her. Elijah and Sasha had just had their first dance, and now everyone was littering the dance floor.

"Of course," Valarie said. He took her into his arms and the two of them began to dance.

The incident at Franko's mansion had taken place one year ago. It was hard to believe that everything had turned out right. Somehow, miraculously, it had. The FBI had been waiting on the other side of the wall. The moment it collapsed, they rushed in. They had been able to help James and find enough evidence at the mansion to criminally charge Franko with life in prison.

"I love you," James whispered, and Valarie smiled, hugging him tightly.

"I love you more," she whispered. She looked around; her heart filled with happiness. Sasha was dancing with Elijah, while Josie and Jack stood in the corner, fussing over their baby.

Terry and Kat stood near the bar, laughing over some joke that Terry had just said. While Jim sat in his wheelchair, holding Hillary's hand as the two of them chatted with Jim's family.

Valarie looked around at all her friends, a huge smile on her face. All her friends had gone through various difficulties in life. Yet all of them had conquered. They now could all look forward to many happy years ahead.

The End.

ABOUT THE AUTHOR

.. ⚘ ..

Ava Axton is a bestselling author of many action-adventure romance novels, known for her ability to captivate readers with heart and soul.

With a colorful life that includes being a wife, mother, former gymnast, actress, musician, and charity voice, Ava finds inspiration in remote resorts and camping trips.

Her stories transport readers to lush, untamed lands where brave, flawed heroes and strong, independent women exist in a world where chivalry still thrives.

Ava's captivating writing style continues to win the hearts of millions worldwide, making her books a must-read for romance fans.

Additional Author Books

- Echoes[1]

- Buried[2]

- Darkness[3]

- Bound[4]

---

1. https://www.amazon.com/dp/B09XP7T1QB

2. https://www.amazon.com/dp/B09XR6QVFF

3. https://www.amazon.com/dp/B09XP4ML7T

4. https://www.amazon.com/dp/B09XPF765B

Leave Me a Review

. . ⚜ . .

If you really enjoyed this book or found it useful, please take a moment to leave a review on Amazon.

I am interested in learning what you like, think, and want.

I read all the reviews personally.

https://www.amazon.com/dp/B09XPKMVF8

Thank you so much for your support!

Don't miss out!

Visit the website below and you can sign up to receive emails whenever Ava Axton publishes a new book. There's no charge and no obligation.

https://books2read.com/r/B-A-EYOR-OZIJC

BOOKS 2 READ

Connecting independent readers to independent writers.

Did you love *LOVE*? Then you should read *Sweet Embrace*[5] by Ava Axton!

[6]

Tales of Love's Trials and Triumphs.........

Step into a world of entangled destinies and heartfelt journeys on our website. Join Sasha as she reunites with her high school flame, Elijah, bound by a hidden secret. Witness Josie's resilience as she faces her past tormentor while carrying his child. Experience the unexpected connection between Terry and Kat, entwined in danger and desire.

Discover the transformative power of love as Hailey and Jim find solace in each other while battling their own demons.

---

5. https://books2read.com/u/mYqK9o

6. https://books2read.com/u/mYqK9o

Unravel the mysteries of the heart with Val and James as they navigate through danger and attraction.

Explore stories of love's endurance, healing, and redemption as these characters confront their trials.

Will love conquer all, or will life's challenges be insurmountable?

Join us and delve into the intricate tapestry of emotions, where love's triumphs shine even in the face of adversity.

Read more at https://www.amazon.com/author/avaaxton.

Also by Ava Axton

Romance Wealth Series
SOJOURN TO THE UNKNOWN
PARAMOUR KING
MAVERICK CROWN
LONG LIVE THE QUEEN
COLOSSUS UNRAVELING
BUTTERFLY RISING

Yearning Series
ECHOES
BURIED
DARKNESS
BOUND
LOVE

Watch for more at https://www.amazon.com/author/avaaxton.

About the Author

Ava Axton is a bestselling author of action-adventure romance novels, known for her ability to captivate readers with heart and soul.

With a colorful life that includes being a wife, mother, former gymnast, actress, musician, and charity voice, Ava finds inspiration in remote resorts and camping trips.

Her stories transport readers to lush, untamed lands where brave, flawed heroes and strong, independent women exist in a world where chivalry still thrives.

Ava's captivating writing style continues to win the hearts of millions worldwide, making her books a must-read for romance fans.

Read more at https://www.amazon.com/author/avaaxton.